Lights, Camera,
CARMEN!

By
ANIKA DENISE

Illustrated by
LORENA ALVAREZ GÓMEZ

Abrams Books for Young Readers
New York

Carmen is a star of the stage . . .

and living room.

After every show, audiences applaud and throw flowers at her feet.

She paces the kitchen, thinking up showstopping ideas.

"In my dinosaur bowl?" suggests Eduardo.

"They'll be expecting that," says Carmen.

"We need something BIG! A showstopper."

"Right," Eduardo agrees. "What's a *showstopper*?"

"Something totally original," says Carmen.

Carmen reads the contest rules. "It says, 'Show the world how you eat your Dino-Krispies.'"

"Can I help?" Eduardo asks.

"Sure, you can be my cinematographer," says Carmen.

"What's a *cinnamon-tographer*?" asks Eduardo.

"Just press Record," says Carmen.

"¿Qué pasa?" asks Carmen's dad.
"I'm going to be in a commercial," Carmen explains.
"Congratulations," says Carmen's mother.

"My destiny!" says Carmen.
"All I have to do is win the
Dino-Krispies contest."

"Hermanito, I've made a decision. I'm taking a break from the theater to pursue a film career."

"What's a *film career?*" asks Eduardo.

"Those aren't rose petals," says Carmen
to her little brother, Eduardo.

"All I could find was cereal."

The cereal box gives
Carmen an idea.

"I've got it!" says Carmen.
"Dino-Krispies **SMOOTHIES!**
It's a totally original way to
eat cereal."

Carmen adds the krispies.
And the milk.
And some pickles.

"Lights! Camera! **ACTION!**"
she shouts.

"Was that a showstopper?"

While rinsing out the sponges and putting away the mop, Carmen mopes. Carmen is a very dramatic moper.

"Why so glum, Glumpelstiltskin?" asks Carmen's dad.
"Because to win the contest, I need something **BIG!**" says Carmen.

"We understand, *mamita*," says
Carmen's mother. "But I think we've
had enough big ideas for today."

"A true artist overcomes rejection," says Carmen.
She puts on her best thinking wings—and *thinks*.

"You know what this commercial needs?" she asks.

"A cinnamon-tographer?" suggests Eduardo.

"A dance number!" says Carmen.
"Ready? Lights! Camera—"
"**ACTION!**" shouts Eduardo.

Carmen's dance number
has sixteen *grand jetés*.
And a tango.
And some jazz hands.

"Want to see me take a
T. rex bite?" Eduardo asks.
"*Shh*," says Carmen. "The
cinematographer can't be
in the commercial."

Eduardo slurps up his milk like
a thirsty stegosaurus.

"*Aaaaand* cut," says Carmen.
"That's a wrap."

Weeks later, a letter arrives . . .

Keller's Corporation

Dear Carmen,

All of us at Keller's Corporation enjoyed your bloopers reel. How clever! But the real showstopper was your adorable little brother in his dinosaur costume.

We'd like to make him the face of our "How Do You Eat YOUR Dino-Krispies?" campaign. Congratulations!

A representative from our advertising agency will be in touch soon.

Sincerely,

Gloria Keller, CEO

When Carmen's dad finishes reading the letter, Carmen is very quiet.
"Are you okay, Carmencita?" asks Carmen's mom.

Carmen stomps off to her dressing room and slams the door.

"Carmen?" Eduardo peeks in. "I decided I don't want to be a showstopper."
"*Hermanito*," Carmen sighs. "Haven't I ever told you the most important rule of show business?"

A little while later, Carmen's dad
brings her a snack.
"Room service! *¿Tienes hambre?*"

"I guess so," Carmen shrugs.
"Your brother made it for
you," says Carmen's dad. "You
know he's your biggest fan.
He didn't mean to steal the
show."

"Don't throw cereal at you?"
"Not that one," says Carmen.
"The most important one is:
The show must go on."

"You won't be mad at me
if I'm in the commercial?"
Eduardo asks.
"No," says Carmen. "It's your
destiny. So you'll do it?"
"Yes!" shouts Eduardo.

"*Hermanito*," says Carmen, "do you know what this means?"

"What?" Eduardo asks.

"You're going to need an **AGENT!**"

FOR ELISA, MI HERMANITA FAVORITA
—A.D.

FOR LILIANA, MY SISTER
—L.A.G.

The illustrations in this book were made with paper, pencils, and Photoshop.

Cataloging-in-Publication Data has been applied for and may be obtained from the Library of Congress.

ISBN 978-1-4197-3169-3

Text copyright © 2018 Anika Denise
Illustrations copyright © 2018 Lorena Alvarez Gómez
Book design by Siobhán Gallagher

Printed and bound in China
10 9 8 7 6 5 4 3 2 1

Abrams Books for Young Readers are available at special discounts when purchased in quantity for premiums and promotions as well as fundraising or educational use. Special editions can also be created to specification. For details, contact specialsales@abramsbooks.com or the address below.

ABRAMS The Art of Books
195 Broadway, New York, NY 10007
abramsbooks.com